NOBODY TOLD JAMAAL

Written by Stephen E. Randall

Illustrated by Todd Pearl

ISBN 978-0-9767189-9-0

©2010 Better Day Publishing, LLC

3695F Cascade Road, #2161

Atlanta, GA 30331

Printed in the USA.

Dedication

In memory of

Dolores R. Randall

(10/15/37 - 9/23/1984)

and

Walter T. Randall

(2/28/34 - 2/20/2009)

Prologue

The audience stood and cheered as James Smith stood to accept the "Man of the Year" award. He was clearly the most qualified, as he had accomplished so much in such a short time. Not only was he more intelligent than anyone around him, but he was also wealthier, more successful and obviously better looking.

"Ladies and Gentlemen," James began as he reflected on the rich history of accomplishment that surrounded his life; "It is with pleasure that I accept this award…"

The class erupted in laughter as, once again, the teacher had to shake Jamaal out of his daydream.

"What do you think, Jamaal?" the teacher asked. "What is the significance of Martin Luther King's 'I Have a Dream' speech?"

"Jamaal knows all about dreaming," a student snickered as the class laughed again.

Jamaal buried his head in his hands and began to wish that this day would be over. How did he get himself in this **predicament** again? It always seemed to happen to him. It seemed like every day, in his history class, this would happen. His mind would drift away. And why not? They never talked about anyone like him. "That's what history is … *HIS Story*," he thought as his mind drifted yet again. He was tired of it. It had to get better … soon.

"Your homework for this evening," the teacher continued, jarring Jamaal from his **reverie**, "is to write a two-page essay using the topic on the board, 'If I could be anyone in the history of the world, who would I be, and why?'"

"Anybody but me," Jamaal **murmured** as he copied the homework assignment, "Anybody but me."

The bell rang denoting the end of the school day and Jamaal packed his backpack and headed out. Still upset at the way the day ended but excited that it was finally over, Jamaal rushed from the school, hopped on his bicycle, and sped home.

When Jamaal arrived at home, he unpacked his books, put a frozen pizza in the oven, and sat down to complete his homework. "Who would I be," Jamaal said out loud as he **pondered** his history assignment.

Looking at his reflection in the table, he thought to himself, "Maybe I'll be a basketball star."

Jamaal dribbles the ball down the court. He fakes left; he fakes right; he slams it home. WHAT A PLAY!!!! THE CROWD GOES WILD!!!!

"But I hate basketball," Jamaal winced. "Okay … football then."

And there goes Jamaal, breaking tackles again.
Can anybody stop this man? TOUCHDOWN!!!!

"Don't like football either." The more he thought about it, he realized that he didn't really like sports at all.

"So what can I do?" he thought to himself, "What's left? I GOT IT!!!," he thought, "I'll be an entertainer."

"Ladies and Gentlemen ... Here he is ... he'll make you laugh; he'll make you swoon; the world's funniest man; the man with the golden voice ... JAMAAL!!!"

"But I can't sing," he frowned.

"Let's face it," he said to himself, "I can't sing or dance, I don't like sports, and I can't tell jokes. What's left? I bet if I were white I could do anything I wanted. In fact, I wish I WERE white. And if I were, I wouldn't even touch anything black. It's not like black people have made any significant contribution to society. Life would be just fine without us. Maybe a little less entertaining, but fine nonetheless.

"Yeah, I wish I were white," he thought as the stress of the day began to catch up with him. "If I could be anyone in the history of world, I would be James Smith. Then I could do anything I wanted to do. I could be great." And with that thought filling his **consciousness**, Jamaal fell fast asleep.

II

Jamaal awoke in a fog. Something was really strange. He felt different but he couldn't quite figure out why. He rose from the couch and stumbled into the bathroom to wash his face. When he finished, he noticed a strange person in the restroom with him.

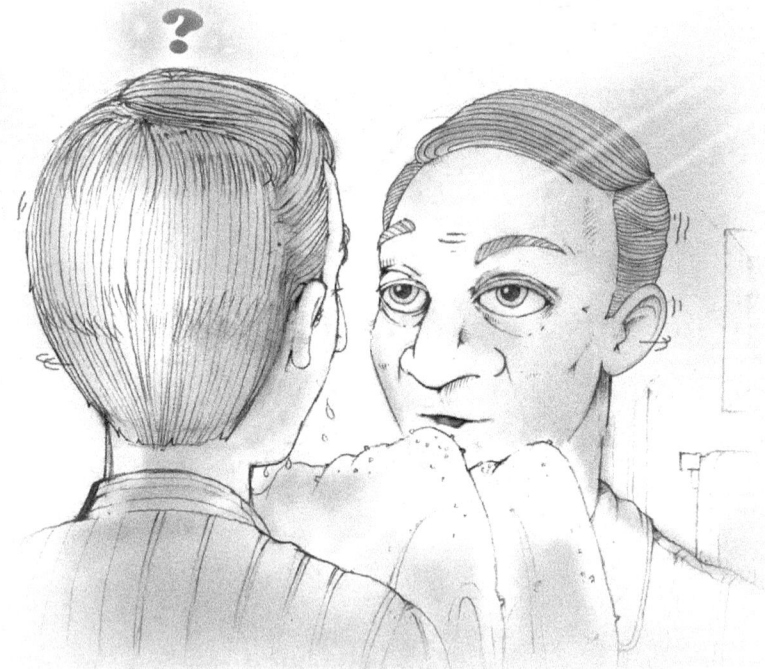

"Who are you?" Jamaal asked. But as he did so, the stranger said exactly the same thing. "I'm not playing with you, what are you doing in my house?" The stranger said the same thing again. "Quit it … I'm not in the mood for games." Same thing again. The stranger was mocking him – mirroring his every move. Jamaal winked; the man winked. Jamaal raised his hand; the man did the same. Jamaal scratched his nose, so did the man.

Suddenly it dawned on him: this wasn't someone mocking Jamaal, It was Jamaal! He had been looking in a mirror the entire time. And

he even knew who this man was. This was James Smith. Of all the things to happen, Jamaal had gotten his wish. He was white. He was James Smith. Life was good!!!!

As he stepped out of the bathroom, Jamaal realized that life was even better than he originally thought. As James Smith, he now lived in the house of his dreams. It was just like the house he had recently seen in the architectural magazine he liked to read. (Too bad as Jamaal he couldn't dream of becoming an architect.) But as James Smith, not only was he white, with unlimited potential, he had a great job (an executive at a multi-site shipping company), a great house (complete with all of the modern technological marvels he had only been able to dream about), and a great car (a convertible sports car – just like the one in the magazine).

But something just wasn't right, James (Jamaal) thought. He couldn't quite put his finger on it, but something just wasn't right. "No bother," he thought as he prepared for his day. He put on a sleek, grey, pin-striped suit and reached for the matching black shoes. For some reason, the closer his hand got to the shoes, the more difficult it was to move his hand. Then, then a strange thing happened. One of the shoes spoke.

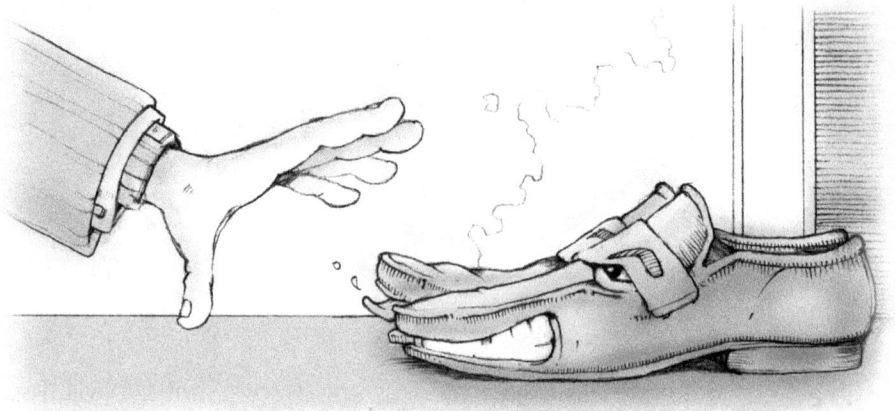

"Jamaal, do you remember what you said? As a condition of your wish, you promised not to touch anything black."

"This is mighty weird," James thought as he reached, instead, for his grey shoes.

"Not black in **hue**," the shoe continued, "An African American man **(the automatic shoe lasting machine was invented by Jan Matzeliger)** was instrumental in my existence. So I'm out of your reach."

James could hardly believe his eyes or his ears. Was a shoe really talking to him? It couldn't be. But sure enough, the more he reached for the shoes, the more he couldn't get them. The only things that James could grab were the sandals that were lying in the corner of the closet. He would look strange, but he had to get to work.

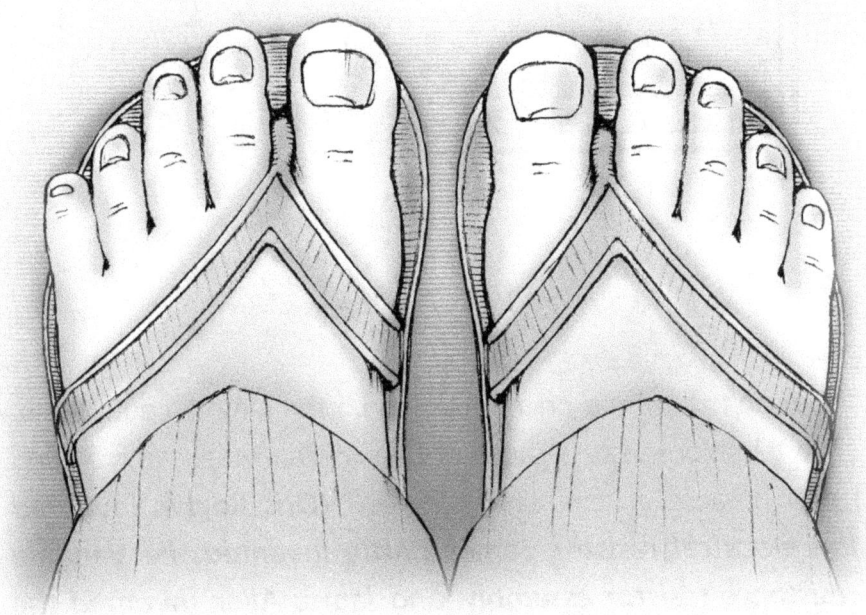

So there he was, freshly **adorned** in his sleek grey suit and sandals. "What a way for the day to start," James thought. "I'd better check the news to see how the traffic is." But before he could reach the remote, sound began to come from the television.

"You can't touch me or the television." the remote control said. "The television exists because of two African American men and I exist because of another Black man" **(Otis Boykin invented the electrical resistor, James Battle invented the variable resistance resistor assembly, and James Allen invented the remote control apparatus).**

"What's going on?" James said aloud. First the shoes – now the television. "This place is strange," he thought, as the **luster** began to wear off of his dream home. "Let me just get out of here and get to work."

On his way out of the door, James reached over to turn off the lights. "Not today," the light switch said. "Black men – Electric Lamp" **(the electric lamp was invented by Lewis Latimer & Joseph Nichols).**

"Okay, enough is enough," James thought as he stepped out of the front door. As he was leaving, he walked down the driveway to the street to drop a letter in the mailbox. Once again, the more he reached for the mailbox, the more his hand shrunk away from it.

"A Black man invented me," the mailbox said **(Phillip B. Downing invented the letter box).** "Remember your conditions."

James was really becoming concerned. This Dream House of his was driving him crazy. Evidently with all of the technological advances in his house, the house could talk to him. "Strange … very strange," he thought.

The more he thought about it, the more he became convinced that had to be it. "It's just technology," he said to himself as he got into his sports car. "I'll figure it out when I get home."

With that, James shifted into first gear, released the clutch, and sped down the street on his way to his office.

III

Arriving at work, James pulled into his parking space and headed towards the building. As he walked into the door, a young lady grabbed his arm from behind. "Mr. Smith, I've been calling you since you got out of the car."

"I'm sorry, I was really pre-occupied," an uneasy James replied.

"Oh, that's ok," the lady continued. "I just wanted to remind you that our meeting has been postponed until this afternoon. Your assistant has the details. I'll see you then."

"I can't let this happen again," he thought to himself. "I've got to remember … my name is James Smith, James Smith, James Smith…"

James headed straight for the elevator, as his office was on the fourth floor, part of the executive suites. "That's right," he thought to himself, "THE EXECUTIVE SUITES: such is **befitting** a man of my stature – the 'Man of the Year' no less."

The closer he got to the elevator, however, the more he felt a pull towards the stairs. Finally, almost unable to move at all, he seemed to hear the elevator speaking to him.

"Where are you going?" the elevator asked. "If you want to get to your office, you'd better head towards those stairs!! You can't ride me because of your vow" **(Alexander Miles invented the elevator).**

"Now how did that elevator know where I was going?" James thought to himself. "This technology is just awesome. I didn't know this stuff existed. Seems like not only can everything talk, but it can **anticipate** your thoughts and movements as well." With that thought filling his mind, he headed for the stairs, climbed three floors, and entered the executive suites.

"Good morning Mr. Smith," everyone seemed to say at once.

"How are you today?"

"Congratulations on your award. You certainly deserved it."

"We're lucky to have you."

Praise seemed to ring out from all corners as James approached his office. He made a special effort to acknowledge everyone as he walked through, certain that he was adored and **revered** by all around him.

When he reached his office, he found that his assistant had already unlocked and opened the door and placed his daily itinerary neatly on his desk. Sitting down in his executive chair, he reflexively reached for the keyboard to the computer on his desk.

"What are you doing?" The computer asked. "You can't touch me. Remember your promise" **(Mark Dean patented technological advances in computer architecture that made the personal computer a possibility).**

Before he could comprehend what was going on, the intercom came to life. "You have a very important call," his assistant said.

But try as he might, he just couldn't put his hands on the phone. ***Exasperated*** and puzzled, he instructed his assistant to take a message.

James stared at the phone in disbelief as the receiver lifted up on its own and began to speak. "You know why you can't use me don't you? Remember your rules. Remember your limits. ***(Granville T. Woods invented a telephone transmitter that was far superior to the one invented by Alexander Graham Bell).***

"I really have to figure out this new technology," James scolded himself. "If I'm going to be here, I can't act as if I don't know anything."

But once again, before he could complete that thought, his assistant came in with the message she had just taken, a small bottle of medicine and a lunch menu.

"The call was from your grandmother," the assistant said. "She wanted to remind you to drop off the arthritis medicine that was delivered yesterday. I also took the liberty of ordering your lunch. Steak sandwiches will be delivered shortly." With that she placed the lunch menu, the arthritis medicine, and the message on James' desk, turned, and retreated from the room.

"Wow," James thought, "What an efficient assistant."

No sooner than he could complete the thought, the bizarre technology started again. The arthritis medicine that his assistant had just brought in suddenly seemed to move far from his reach.

"You can't touch me either," the medication said. "Same rules, same story" *(a method for producing affordable Cortisone was invented by Percy Julian).*

"WHAT STORY," James said aloud. "What is this technology talking about? What is really going on?"

Before he could figure it out, his assistant rushed back into the room. This time she was holding an envelope, a book, and a small bag in one hand and pulling a piece of rolling luggage with the other.

"We just got a call from the corporate office," she said. It seems that the Washington, DC and Chicago, IL offices both had system crashes this morning. They want you to take the next flight to Chicago, and once done there head straight to Washington, DC. Here is a flight schedule for the corporate jet and also I've brought in your emergency bag. You can place what you need in it and I will make the necessary arrangements.

"Also lunch was delivered. Here is your steak sandwich, just as you like it. There are drinks in the refrigerator and I've placed the latest novel you were reading, The Three Musketeers, next to the bag with your sandwich." With that, she turned and left.

And then it happened. All at once, James' world seemed to spiral out of control. It suddenly seemed as if everything in the room came alive at once.

"You can't go to Chicago," came out of one corner *(Jean Baptiste Pointe du Sable was the first settler in what is now known as Chicago, IL).*

"DC either," came from another *(Benjamin Banneker produced the surveying plans for the city of Washington, DC).*

"You can't eat me," the sandwich declared, as it seemed to jump from the bag and fly across the room *(Lloyd Augustus Hall invented meat curing salts).*

"You can't read me," the novel affirmed as it flew to yet another corner of the room *(Alexandre Dumas is the author of The Three Musketeers).*

"You can't use me either," the refrigerator shouted as it tightened the seal on its doors *(John Standard patented an improved refrigerator).*

James **recoiled** in fear, finally seeing that this was more than just technology. These things were speaking to him, and only to him. "What is it that they keep talking about?" he asked himself. "I know it's something but I just can't seem to remember."

"WOOP, WOOP, WOOP, WOOP, WOOP," the building alarm blared. "Please be advised, THIS IS NOT A DRILL. I repeat, THIS IS NOT A DRILL!!!! There has been a chemical spill in the basement. Emergency services are in route and we are asking all employees to shelter in place. Please utilize the emergency safety goggles and gas inhalator located in each office. We will update you as more information becomes available."

Just then, **acrid** smoke began to pour into his office through the air vents. James, eyes watering and chest heaving, rushed to the emergency cabinet. He opened the cabinet and reached for the goggles and gas mask as instructed. But just as before, the closer his hand got to the goggles and gas mask, the more difficult it was to move.

"Not again," James cried aloud. "Not now, I can't afford not to know this technology right now. I really need these items."

"You can't touch either one of us," the gas mask said. "Do you remember what you said? You said that if you were white, you wouldn't touch anything black. That's why you can't touch me. I was created by a black man. And so was everything else that has been speaking to you today. Your rules ... your wish ... your story"
(Garrett Morgan invented the gas mask; Powell Johnson invented an eye protector).

It was like someone finally removed the scales from his mind. He began to remember his day and how each of these items would move away from him or not allow him to touch them. His shoes, the lights, the radio, the television, the mailbox, the telephone, the computer, each invented or improved somehow by black persons. And now, the very things he needs to stay alive, he couldn't touch.

"Please help me," James cried, as smoke continued to fill the room. As he began to fade out from the smoke, James, barely able to speak, whispered "Nobody told me."

Suddenly he felt himself falling towards the floor. He reached out for something to stem his fall but nothing was there. The last thing he remembered was the floor rising to meet him as his world became darker and darker.

"Nobody told me," he whispered again as he choked from the fumes. "Nobody told me …"

Jamaal was extremely disoriented as he raised himself from the floor. The smoke alarm was blaring, the room was filled with smoke and, for some reason, he found himself groping around for safety goggles and a gas mask. He felt papers all over the floor and finally his hand brushed against something hard.

He pulled himself closer until he began to recognize the item he had grasped hold of: it was his coffee table. He slowly was able to pull himself up from the floor and stumble to the source of the smoke.

The oven!!! Now he remembered. He had placed a frozen pizza in the oven before he sat down to complete his homework. Long since forgotten, the pizza had burned and filled the kitchen and part of the house with smoke.

He quickly removed the burned pizza from the oven, carried it outside to the garbage, and opened several windows to air the house out.

"Whew," he said aloud, "that was a close one." As he slowly began to calm down, he began to remember.

Shoes ... the television ... the remote control ... the electric lamp ... the mailbox ... the elevator ... the personal computer ... the telephone ... arthritis medicine ... Chicago ... Washington, DC ... curing salts for meat ... <u>The Three Musketeers</u> ... the refrigerator ... the gas mask ... safety goggles ... all invented, improved, or discovered by African Americans.

"I guess I was wrong after all," he thought to himself. "History is not just *His Story* but *My Story* as well."

With that thought, he picked up his pen and paper, and began to write.

> *If I could be anyone in the history of the world,*
> *I would be me, a young, strong black man, from*
> *a rich and powerful heritage ...*

—Appendices—

Vocabulary

Acrid
adjective – sharp or biting to the taste or smell; bitterly pungent; irritating to the eyes, nose, etc.
Acrid smoke began to pour into his office.

Adorn
transitive verb – adorned, adorning, adorns – To enhance or decorate with or as if with ornaments:
He was freshly adorned in a sleek grey suit.

Anticipate
verb – to answer (a question), obey (a command), or satisfy (a request) before it is made:
Not only can it talk, but it can also anticipate my thoughts.

Befitting
adjective – suitable; proper; becoming: planned with a befitting sense of majesty.
Such is befitting a man of my stature.

Consciousness
noun – the thoughts and feelings, collectively, of an individual or aggregate of people.
With that thought filling his consciousness, Jamaal fell asleep.

Exasperate
adjective – to irritate or provoke to a high degree; annoy extremely.
Jamaal was exasperated because he couldn't reach the telephone.

Hue
noun – a gradation or variety of a color; tint.
Not black in hue, but black in design.

Luster
adjective – radiance of beauty, excellence, merit, distinction, or glory.
As reality set in, the luster began to wear off of his dream home.

Murmur
verb – to complain in a low tone or in private.
"Anybody but me," Jamaal murmured.

Ponder
verb – to weigh carefully in the mind; consider thoughtfully.
Jamaal pondered his history assignment.

Vocabulary

Predicament   *noun* – an unpleasantly difficult, perplexing, or dangerous situation.
How did he get himself in this predicament again?

Recoil   *intransitive verb* – To shrink back, as in fear or repugnance
James recoiled in fear.

Revere   *verb* – to regard with respect tinged with awe; venerate.
He was revered by all around him.

Reverie   *noun* – A state of dreamy meditation or fanciful musing
The teacher jarred Jamaal from his reverie.

Inventions and Inventors

Automatic Shoe Lasting Machine
March 20, 1883, patent # 274,207

Jan E. Matzeliger

Electrical Resistor
February 21, 1961, patent # 2,972,726

Otis F. Boykin

Variable Resistance Resistor Assembly
September 12, 1972, patent # 3,691,503

James Battle

Remote Control Apparatus
June 29, 1937, # 2,085,624

James Allen

Electric Lamp
September 13, 1881, Patent # 247,097

Lewis Latimer &
Joseph Nichols

Letter Box
October 27, 1891, Patent # 462,092

Phillip B. Downing

Elevator
October 11, 1887, Patent #371,207

Alexander Miles

Improvements in Computer Architecture
August 9, 1985, patent # 4,528,626

Mark Dean

Inventions and Inventors

Telephone Transmitter   Granville T. Woods
December 2, 1884, patent # 308,817

Preparation of Cortisone   Percy Julian
June 26, 1956, patent # 2,752,339

First Settler in Chicago, IL   Jean Baptiste
                                                    Pointe du Sable

Surveying Plans for Washington, DC   Benjamin Banneker

Meat Curing Salt Composition   Lloyd Augustus Hall
November 27, 1956, patent # 2,770,551

The Three Musketeers   Alexandre Dumas
Serialized March – July, 1844

Refrigerator   John Standard
July 14, 1891, patent # 455,891

Gas Mask   Garrett A. Morgan
October 13, 1914, patent # 1,113,675

Eye Protector   Powell Johnson
November 2, 1880, patent # 234,039

Biographies of Selected Inventors

Otis F. Boykin
Electrical Resistor
February 21, 1961 – patent #2,972,726

Otis F. Boykin was born on August 29, 1920 in Dallas, Texas. After graduating high school, he attended Fisk College in Nashville, Tennessee. He graduated in 1941 and took a job as a laboratory assistant with the Majestic Radio and TV Corporation in Chicago, Illinois. He undertook various tasks but excelled at testing automatic aircraft controls, ultimately serving as a supervisor. Three years laster he left Majestic and took a position as a research engineer with the P.J. Nilsen Research Laboratories. Soon thereafter, he decided to try to develop a business of his own a founded Boykin-Fruth, Incorporated. At the same time, he decided to continue his education, pursuing graduate studies at the Illinois Institute of Technology in Chicago, Illinois. He attended classes in 1946 and 1947 but was forced to drop out because he lacked the funds to pay the next year's tuition.

Despite this setback, Boykin realized that a Masters Degree was not a pre-requisite for inventive competence. He set out to work on project that he had contemplated while in school. At the time, the field of electronics was very popular among the science community and Boykin took a special interest in working with resistors. A resistor is an electronic component that slows the flow of an electrical current. This is necessary to prevent too much electricity from passing through a component than is necessary or even safe. Boykin sought and received a patent for a wire precision resistor on June 16, 1959. This resistor allowed for specific amounts of current to flow through for a specific purpose and would be used in radios and televisions. Two years later, he created another resistor that could be manufactured very inexpensively. It was a break-through device as it could withstand extreme changes in temperature and tolerate and withstand various levels of pressure and physical trauma without impairing its effectiveness. The chip was cheaper and more reliable than others on the market. Not surprisingly, it was in great demand as he received orders from consumer electronics manufacturers, the United States military and electronics behemoth IBM.

In 1964, Boykin moved to Paris, creating electronic innovations for a new market of customers. Most of these creations involved electrical resistance components (including small component thick-film resistors used in computers and variable resistors used in guided missile systems) but he also created other important products including a chemical air filter and a burglarproof cash register. His most famous invention, however, was a control unit for the pacemaker, which used electrical impulses to stimulate the heart and create a steady heartbeat. In a tragic irony, Boykin died in 1982 as a result of heart failure.

Otis Boykin proved that the setback of having to drop out of school was not enough to deter him from his dream of becoming an inventor and having a long-lasting effect on the world.

Biographies of Selected Inventors

Dr. Mark Dean

Improvements in Computer Architecture
August 9, 1985 – patent # 4,528,626

Mark Dean's grandfather was a high school principal and his father was a supervisor at the TVA (Tennessee Valley Authority) Dam. One of the few African American students attending his Jefferson City (Tenn.) High School, he was both a star athlete and a straight-A student. In 1979 he graduated at the top of his class at the University of Tennessee though he was actually a part of the university's Minority Engineering Program.

After integration, he recalls, one white friend in sixth grade asked if he was really black. Dean said his friend had concluded he was too smart to be black.

"That was the problem -- the assumption about what blacks could do was tilted," Dean said.

That was the same bias Dean said he encountered when he first joined IBM, and a problem that has not completely disappeared.

"A lot of kids growing up today aren't told that you can be whatever you want to be," he said. "There may be obstacles, but there are no limits."

Dean has been with IBM since 1980. Dean holds 3 of the original 9 patents on the computer that all PCs are based upon: Soon after joining IBM, Dean and a colleague, Dennis Moeller, developed the interior architecture (ISA systems bus) that enables multiple devices, like modem and printer, to be connected to personal computers. Then he worked for a number of years before considering the doctorate.

Dr. Dean has said "when I was accepted at Stanford I had been out of school for ten years, so it was very difficult. I encourage people to go on to graduate school, but they should not wait as long as I did. It makes it very hard, But for me it was definitely the right thing to do and Stanford was the right place to do it. In hindsight, Stanford was the best choice because I already knew what I wanted to work on and both David Dill and then Mark Horowitz enthusiastically supported me in pursuing the research topic I wanted to work on. The research I engaged in as a graduate student was very prudent, in that while some of the technology isn't necessarily what we are doing today, it did allow me to better understand the best ways (pros and cons of certain approaches) to approach the development of processes. I came to Stanford with no knowledge of either circuits or processes, I knew logic design, architectures, bus interfaces and protocol, but I had no real knowledge of transistors, silicon processes and circuits. Stanford was my first exposure to custom circuits design and to building things at transistor level. I am now managing a group focused on high-speed circuit design and I couldn't have done it without the background I received at Stanford."

He earned his Ph.D. in Electrical Engineering in 1992.

Dr. Dean was named an IBM Fellow in 1995, one of only 50 active fellows of IBM's 300,000 employees. Dean was the first African American to be honored with the IBM Fellowship.

Biographies of Selected Inventors

In 1997 Dean was inducted into the National Inventors Hall of Fame for inventing "a system that has allowed PCs to become part of our lives." In 1999, as Director of IBM's Austin Research Lab (in Austin, Texas), he lead the team that built a gigahertz (1000 MHz) chip which did a billion calculations per second. In 2001 he was elected member of the National Academy of Engineers (NAE). In 2004, Dr. Dean was selected as one of the 50 Most Important Blacks in Research Science.

Biographies of Selected Inventors

Alexandre Dumas
Author, The Three Musketeers
Serialized March – July, 1844

Alexandre Dumas was born on July 24, 1802, in the town of Villers-Cotterêts in France. He was the son of Thomas-Alexandre Dumas, a French General, and of Marie-Louise Élisabeth Labouret, the daughter of an innkeeper. His father was himself the son of the Marquis Alexandre-Antoine Davy de la Pailleterie, who served the government of France as Général commissaire in the Artillery in the colony of Saint-Domingue (now part of Haiti), and his black slave Marie-Césette Dumas. This made Alexandre Dumas a quarter black.

General Dumas died in 1806 when Alexandre was not yet four years old, leaving a nearly impoverished mother to raise him under difficult conditions. Although Marie-Louise was unable to provide her son with much in the way of education, it did not hinder young Alexandre's love of books, and he read everything he could get his hands on.

Growing up, his mother's stories of his father's brave military deeds during the glory years of Napoleon I of France spawned Alexandre's vivid imagination for adventure and heroes. Although poor, the family still had the father's distinguished reputation and aristocratic connections, and after the restoration of the monarchy, twenty-year-old Alexandre Dumas moved to Paris where he obtained employment at the Palais Royal in the office of the powerful duc d'Orléans.

While working in Paris, Dumas began to write articles for magazines as well as plays for the theatre. In 1829 his first solo play, Henry III and his

Court, was produced, meeting with great public acclaim. The following year his second play, Christine, proved equally popular, and as a result, he was financially able to work full time at writing. In 1830, he participated in the revolution that ousted King Charles X and replaced him on the throne with Dumas's former employer, the duc d'Orléans, who would rule as Louis-Philippe, the Citizen King.

After writing more successful plays, he turned his efforts to novels. Although attracted to an extravagant lifestyle, and always spending more than he earned, Dumas proved to be a very astute business marketer. With high demand from newspapers for serial novels, in 1838, he simply rewrote one of his plays to create his first serial novel. Titled Le Capitaine Paul, it led to his forming a production studio that turned out hundreds of stories, all subject to his personal input and direction.

Despite Alexandre Dumas' success and aristocratic connections, his being of mixed-race would affect him all his life. In 1843, he wrote a short novel, Georges that addressed some of the issues of race and the effects of colonialism. Nevertheless, racist attitudes impacted his rightful position in France's history long after his death on December 5, 1870, at the age of 68.

Buried in the place where he had been born, Alexandre Dumas remained in the cemetery at Villers-Cotterêts until November 30, 2002. Under orders of the French President, Jacques Chirac, his body was exhumed, and in a televised ceremony, his new coffin, draped in a blue-velvet cloth and flanked by four Republican Guards costumed as the Musketeers - Athos, Porthos, Aramis, and D'Artagnan - was transported in a solemn procession to the Panthéon of Paris, the great mausoleum where French luminaries are interred.

In his speech, President Chirac said: "With you, we were D'Artagnan, Monte Cristo, or Balsamo, riding along the roads of France, touring battlefields, visiting palaces and castles – with you, we dream." In an interview following the ceremony, President Chirac acknowledged the racism that had existed, saying that a wrong had now been righted with Alexandre Dumas enshrined alongside fellow authors Victor Hugo and Voltaire.

The honor recognized that although France has produced many great writers, none have been as widely read as Alexandre Dumas. His stories have been translated into almost a hundred languages, and have inspired more than 200 motion pictures.

Jean Baptiste Pointe du Sable

First Settler in Chicago, IL

Circa 1780's

Jean Baptiste Pointe du Sable was the first known settler in the area which is now Chicago, Illinois. He was long ignored by historians, partly because he was a Haitian and not fully white, and partly because the early histories were written by the friends and descendants of John Kinzie, to whom du Sable sold his house in 1800.

Little is known for sure about du Sable's early life. He may have been born as early as the 1730s to a slave named Suzanna and a French pirate mate named Pointe du Sable who served about the Black Sea Gull. Suzanna may have been killed in a Spanish raid on Haiti, and perhaps Jean Baptiste escaped by swimming out to his father's ship. After his father sent him to study at a Catholic school in France, du Sable and a friend, Jacques Clamorgan, traveled to Louisiana and then to Michigan, where du Sable married the Potawatomi Kittihawa.

Du Sable built his first house in Chicago in the 1770s on the land now known as Pioneer Court, thirty years before Fort Dearborn was established on the banks of the Chicago River. By the time he sold to Kinzie's front man, Jean La Lime, for 6,000 livres, his property included a house, two barns, a horse mill, a bake house, a poultry house, a dairy and a smokehouse. The interior was richly appointed as well. His home also served as the first trading post in Chicago.

In 1800 du Sable left Chicago for Peoria, and in 1805 headed to Missouri. He died in St. Charles, and was buried in an unmarked grave in

St. Borromeo Cemetery until a granite marker was erected in 1968. His home in Missouri eventually became the official residence of the first governor of Missouri.

Biographies of Selected Inventors

Lloyd Augustus Hall
Meat Curing Salt Composition
November 27, 1956 – patent # 2,770,551

Lloyd Augustus Hall was born on June 20, 1894 in Elgin, Illinois. He was an honor student while attending West Side High School in Aurora, Illinois and captained the school debate team while competing in baseball, football and track. Lloyd graduated High School in the top 10 of his class and had to choose between four college scholarship offers. He decided to attend nearby Northwestern University, earning a Bachelor Degree in Pharmaceutical Chemistry in 1916.

While at Northwestern, Hall attended classes with a fellow student named Carroll L. Griffith who would later go on to become the founder of Griffith Laboratories. After graduation, Hall earned a graduate degree from the University of Chicago.

Hall was soon hired by the Western Electric Company through a telephone interview. When he showed up for his first day, however, he was told by a personnel officer that "we don't take niggers." Recovering from this slight, he began working for the Chicago Department of Health as a chemist and was promoted in 1917 to senior chemist. The next year he moved to Ottumwa, Iowa where he held the position of chief chemist at the John Morrell Company. During this time, World War I broke out and Hall received an appointment as Chief Inspector of Powder and Explosives for the United States Ordnance Department.

On September 23, 1919 Lloyd married Myrrhene Newsome, a teacher from Macomb, Illinois. Two years later, the couple moved to Chicago where Lloyd began working for the Boyer Chemical Laboratory where he took the position of chief chemist and focused on the emerging field of food chemistry, and began looking at a way of preserving meats with chemicals. In 1922 he moved on to Chemical Products Corporation where he served as President and Chemical director of their consulting laboratory and often consulted with Griffith Laboratories. In 1925, Hall was offered a position with Griffith Laboratories as chief chemist and director of research. Griffith Laboratories, of course, had been founded by Hall's former classmate Carroll Griffith and after years of moving from company to company, Hall accepted the position and remained there for the next 34 years.

Hall had been working for a number of years exploring different areas of food chemistry and upon joining Griffith Laboratories began looking into methods for preserving foods. Up to that point, foods, and especially meats had been preserved by using sodium chloride (table salt). Hall found a way of encasing nitrates and nitrites within a sodium chloride "shell" by utilizing a process called "flash-drying" crystals over heated rollers. This allowed sodium nitrate to be introduced to the meats first and dissolved, and then nitrates and nitrites were able to penetrate the "preserved" meat and therefore "cure" it.

Hall also maintained an interest in sterilizing foods, utensils and tools. Although many people thought that certain spices and flavorings also had the added benefit of preserving foods, Hall found that many of these agents actually exposed the foods to an abundance of germs, molds and bacteria. Hall set out to prevent this while at the same time allowing the spices and flavorings to retain the aroma and color. He eventually found a gas called ethylene oxide, which he introduced to the foods within a vacuumed environment which eliminated the germs and bacteria while maintaining appearances, taste and aroma.

These contributions to food preservation and sterilization revolution-ized the way foods were processed, prepared, packed and transported, eliminating spoilage and health hazards and improving efficiency and profitability for food suppliers. In the course of his work, Hall would publish more than 5 scientific papers and receive more than 100 patents. He also served as an advisor to the United States during two World Wars, served on dozens of advisory panels and boards and received hundreds of awards and accolades.

In 1959 Hall retired from Griffith Laboratories and moved to Pasadena, California where he died in 1971. He left behind a legacy as a pioneer in the field of food chemistry and is responsible for improving health conditions in all areas of the food industry.

Percy Julian
Preparation of Cortisone
June 26, 1956 – patent # 2,752,339

Percy Julian was born on April 11, 1899 in Birmingham, Alabama, one of six children. His father, a railroad mail clerk, and his mother, a school teacher stressed education to their children. This emphasis would ultimately prove successful as two sons went on to become physicians and three daughters would receive Masters Degrees, but it was son Percy who would become the most successful of the children.

Percy attended elementary school in Birmingham and moved on to Montgomery, Alabama where he attended high school at the State Normal School for Negroes. Upon graduation in 1916, Julian applied to and was accepted into DePauw University in Greencastle, Indiana. At DePauw, he began as a probationary student, having to take higher level high school classes along with his freshman and sophomore course load. Finally, upon graduation from DePauw in 1920, he was selected as the class valedictorian. Though at the top of his classes, he was discouraged from seeking admission into a graduate school because of potential racial sentiment on the part of future coworkers and employers. Instead, he took the advice of an advisor and took a position as a chemistry teacher at Fisk University, a Black college in Nashville, Tennessee.

After two years at Fisk, Julian was awarded the Austin Fellowship in Chemistry and moved to the distinguished Harvard University in Cambridge, Massachusetts. He achieved straight A's, finishing at the top of his class and receiving a Masters Degree in 1923. Even with this success, Julian was unable to obtain a position as a teaching assistant at any major universities because of the perception that White students would refuse to learn under a Black instructor. Thus, he moved on to a teaching position at West Virginia State College for Negroes. He left West Virginia and served as an associate professor of chemistry at Howard University in Washington, D.C. for two years.

In 1929, Julian qualified for and received a Fellowship from the General Education Board and traveled to Vienna, Austria in pursuit of a Ph.D. degree. While in Vienna, Julian developed a fascination with the soybean and its interesting properties and capabilities. Julian received his Ph.D. in 1931 and returned to Howard University as the head of the school's chemistry department. He soon left Howard and moved back to DePauw where he was appointed a teacher in organic chemistry. At DePauw, he worked with an associate of his from Vienna, Dr. Josef Pikl, on the synthesis of physostigmine, a drug which was used as a treatment for glaucoma. After much work and adversity, Julian was successful and became internationally hailed for his achievement. At this point the Dean of the University sought to appoint Julian to the position as Chair of the chemistry department but was talked out of it by others in the department, again because of concerns over reaction to his race.

In late 1935, Percy Julian decided to leave the world of academics and entered the corporate world by accepting a position with the Glidden Company as chief chemist. This was a significant development as he was the first Black scientist hired for such a position and would pave the way for other Blacks in the future.

Biographies of Selected Inventors

On December 24, 1935, Percy married Anna Johnson and the couple settled into their comfortable life in Chicago. Percy continued his success as he next developed a way to inexpensively develop male and female hormones from soy beans. These hormones would help to prevent miscarriages in pregnant women and would be used to fight cancer and other ailments. He next set out to provide a synthetic version of cortisone, a product which greatly relieved the pain of suffered by sufferers of rheumatoid arthritis. The real cortisone was extremely expensive and only rich people could afford it. With Julian's discovery of the soy-based substitute, millions of sufferers around the world found relief at a reasonable price. So significant was his work that in 1950 the City of Chicago named him Chicagoan of the Year. While the honor should have signaled Julian's acceptance by his white counterparts in his field and his community, when he soon after purchased a home for his family in nearby Oak Park, some residents of the town still could not stand to have him as their neighbor simply because he was Black.

In 1954, Julian left the Glidden Company to establish Julian Laboratories which specialized in producing his synthetic cortisone. In 1961 he sold the Oak Park plant to Smith, Kline and French, a giant pharmaceutical company and received a sum of 2.3 million dollars, a staggering amount for a Black man at that time.

Biographies of Selected Inventors

Jan Matzeliger

Automatic Shoe Lasting Machine

March 20, 1883 – patent # 274,207

Jan Matzeliger was born in Dutch Guiana (now known as Surinam) in South America. His father was a Dutch engineer and his mother was born in Dutch Guiana and was of African ancestry. His father had been sent to Surinam by the Dutch government to oversee the work going on in the South American country.

At an early age, Jan showed a remarkable ability to repair complex machinery and often did so when accompanying his father to a factory. When he turned 19, he decided to venture away from home to explore other parts of the world. For two years he worked aboard an East Indian merchant ship and was able to visit several countries. In 1873, Jan decided to stay in the United States for a while, landing in Pennsylvania. Although he spoke very little English, he was befriended by some Black residents who were active in a local church and took pity on him. Because he was good with his hands and mechanically inclined, he was able to get small jobs in order to earn a living.

At some point he began working for a cobbler and became interested in the making of shoes. At that time more than half of the shoes produced in the United States came from the small town of Lynn, Massachusetts. Still unable to speak more than rudimentary English, Matzeliger had a difficult time finding work in Lynn. After considerable time, he was able to begin working as a show apprentice in a shoe factory. He operated a McKay sole-sewing machine which was used to attach different parts of a shoe together. Unfortunately, no machines existed that could attach the upper part of a shoe to the sole. As such, attaching the upper part of a shoe to the sole had to be done by hand. The people who were able to sew the parts of the shoe together were called "hand lasters" and expert ones were able to produce about 50 pairs of shoes in a 10 hour work day.

After working all day Matzeliger took classes at night to learn English. Soon, he was able to read well enough to study books on physics and mechanical science

Soon, Matzeliger began putting together a crude working model of an invention which would imitate the mannerisms of hand lasters. As he improved the device, offers of money came in, some as high as $1,500.00. Matzeliger could not bear to part with the device he had put so much work into creating so he held out until he reached a deal to sell a 66% interest in the devices to two investors, retaining the other third interest for himself. With the new influx of cash, Jan finished his second and third models of the machine. At this point he applied for a patent for the device.

Because no one could believe that anyone could create a machine which could duplicate the work of expert lasters, the patent office dispatched a representative to Lynn, Massachusetts to see the device in action. In March 1883, the United States Patent Office issued a patent to Jan Matzeliger for his "Lasting Machine." Within two years, Matzeliger had perfected the machine to that point that it could produce up to 700 pairs of shoes each day.

Sadly, Matzeliger would only enjoy his success for a short time, as he was afflicted with tuberculosis in 1886 and died on August 24, 1889 at the age of 37. As a result of his work, shoe manufacturing capabilities increased as did efficiency. This allowed for lower prices for consumers and more jobs for workers. Matzeliger left behind a legacy of tackling what was thought to be an impossible task - making shoes affordable for the masses.

Biographies of Selected Inventors

Garrett A. Morgan
Safety Hood and Smoke Protector (Gas Mask)
October 13, 1914 – patent # 1,113,675

Garrett Morgan was an inventor and businessman from Cleveland who invented a device called the Morgan safety hood and smoke protector in 1914. On July 25, 1916, Garrett Morgan made national news for using his gas mask to rescue 32 men trapped during an explosion in an underground tunnel 250 feet beneath Lake Erie. Morgan and a team of volunteers donned the new "gas masks" and went to the rescue. After the rescue, Morgan's company received requests from fire departments around the country who wished to purchase the new masks. The Morgan gas mask was later refined for use by U.S. Army during World War I. In 1914, Garrett Morgan was awarded a patent for a Safety Hood and Smoke Protector. Two years later, a refined model of his early gas mask won a gold medal at the International Exposition of Sanitation and Safety, and another gold medal from the International Association of Fire Chiefs.

The son of former slaves, Garrett Morgan was born in Paris, Kentucky on March 4, 1877. His early childhood was spent attending school and working on the family farm with his brothers and sisters. While still a teenager, he left Kentucky and moved north to Cincinnati, Ohio in search of opportunity.

Although Garrett Morgan's formal education never took him beyond elementary school, he hired a tutor while living in Cincinnati and continued his studies in English grammar. In 1895, Morgan moved to

Biographies of Selected Inventors

Cleveland, Ohio, where he went to work as a sewing machine repair man for a clothing manufacturer. News of his proficiency for fixing things and experimenting traveled fast and led to numerous job offers from various manufacturing firms in the Cleveland area.

The first American-made automobiles were introduced to U.S. consumers shortly before the turn of the century. The Ford Motor Company was founded in 1903 and with it American consumers began to discover the adventures of the open road. In the early years of the 20th century it was not uncommon for bicycles, animal-powered wagons, and new gasoline-powered motor vehicles to share the same streets and roadways with pedestrians. Accidents were frequent. After witnessing a collision between an automobile and a horse-drawn carriage, Garrett Morgan took his turn at inventing a traffic signal. Other inventors had experimented with, marketed, and even patented traffic signals, however, Garrett Morgan was one of the first to apply for and acquire a U.S. patent for an inexpensive to produce traffic signal. The patent was granted on November 20, 1923. Garrett Morgan also had his invention patented in Great Britain and Canada.

Garrett Morgan's hand-cranked semaphore traffic management device was in use throughout North America until all manual traffic signals were replaced by the automatic red, yellow, and green-light traffic signals currently used around the world. The inventor sold the rights to his traffic signal to the General Electric Corporation for $40,000. Shortly before his death in 1963, Garrett Morgan was awarded a citation for his traffic signal by the United States Government.

Biographies of Selected Inventors

Garrett Morgan was constantly experimenting to develop new concepts. Though the traffic signal came at the height of his career and became one of his most renowned inventions, it was just one of several innovations he developed, manufactured, and sold over the years.

Garrett Morgan died on August 27, 1963, at the age of 86. His life was long and full, and his creative energies have given us a marvelous and lasting legacy.

Biographies of Selected Inventors

John Standard
Refrigerator

July 14, 1891 – patent # 455,891

An improved refrigerator design was patented by African American inventor John Standard of Newark, NJ. John Standard was also granted U.S. patent #413,689 on 10/29/1889 for an oil stove.

In his patent for the refrigerator John Standard declared, "This invention relates to improvements in refrigerators; and it consists of certain novel arrangements and combinations of parts." This means that John Standard was saying that he had found a way to improve the design of a refrigerator that he looked at an existing refrigerator and made it better.

Contrary to popular folklore John Standard did not invent the very first refrigerator, however, every patent represents something that has not be done before and most utility patents are issued for what is called an "improvement." Improvements are the work of inventors and often it is the improved design that succeeds.

Granville T. Woods

Telephone Transmitter

December 2, 1884 – patent # 308,817

Born in Columbus, Ohio, in April 23, 1856, Granville T. Woods dedicated his life to developing a variety of inventions relating to the railroad industry. To some he was known as the "Black Edison, both great inventors of their time. Granville T. Woods invented more than a dozen devices to improve electric railway cars and many more for controlling the flow of electricity. His most noted invention was a system for letting the engineer of a train know how close his train was to others. This device helped cut down accidents and collisions between trains.

Granville T. Woods literally learned his skills on the job. Attending school in Columbus until age 10, he served an apprenticeship in a machine shop and learned the trades of machinist and blacksmith. During his youth he also went to night school and took private lessons. Although he had to leave formal school at age ten, Granville T. Woods realized that learning and education were essential to developing critical skills that would allow him to express his creativity with machinery.

In 1888, Granville T. Woods developed a system for overhead electric conducting lines for railroads, which aided in the development of the overhead railroad system found in cities such as Chicago, St. Louis, and New York City. In his early thirties, he became interested in thermal power and steam-driven engines. And, in 1889, he filed his first patent for an improved steam-boiler furnace. In 1892, a complete Electric Railway System was operated at Coney Island, NY. In 1887, he patented the Synchronous Multiplex Railway Telegraph, which allowed communications between train stations from moving trains. Granville T. Woods' invention made it possible for trains to communicate with the station and with other trains so they knew exactly where they were at all times.

Alexander Graham Bell's company purchased the rights to Granville T. Woods' "telegraphony," enabling him to become a full-time inventor. Among his other top inventions were a steam boiler furnace and an automatic air brake used to slow or stop trains. Wood's electric car was powered by overhead wires. It was the third rail system to keep cars running on the right track.

Success led to law suits filed by Thomas Edison who sued Granville Woods claiming that he was the first inventor of the multiplex telegraph. Granville Woods eventually won, but Edison didn't give up easily when he wanted something. Trying to win Granville Woods over, and his inventions, Edison offered Granville Woods a prominent position in the engineering department of Edison Electric Light Company in New York. Granville T. Woods, preferring his independence, declined.

Illustrated by Todd Pearl

Todd Pearl is an accomplished freelance illustrator and designer who happens to be Creative Director and illustrator for Better Day Publishing. He has illustrated many children's books, and currently working on one of his own. Todd resides in Clawson, MI, just outside of Detroit with his wife, Lisa and their two dachshunds, Stella and Cooper.

www.ingramcontent.com/pod-product-compliance
Lightning Source LLC
Chambersburg PA
CBHW080836250626
47160CB00008B/2952